This book belongs to

_____

VOLUME
18

POOH
PLANS A PARTY

WALT DISNEY FUN-TO-READ LIBRARY

A BANTAM BOOK
TORONTO • NEW YORK • LONDON • SYDNEY • AUCKLAND

Winnie the Pooh sat on his doorstep. His friend Piglet was with him. So was Eeyore, the old gray donkey.

"I wonder about birthdays sometimes," said Eeyore. "Perhaps that is because I don't have one."

"You don't have a birthday?" cried Piglet.
"Everyone has a birthday," said Pooh.
"I had one once," said Eeyore. "It was
the day I was born. But I was so little that I
do not remember when that was." Eeyore
walked away then. He looked very sad.

"Poor Eeyore!" said Pooh. "No wonder he is gloomy. Let's cheer him up. Let's give him a birthday party."

"How can we do that?" asked Piglet. "We don't know when his birthday is."

"His birthday might be today," said Pooh. "Who can say that it isn't?"

"What a clever bear you are," said Piglet.

The two friends skipped over to see
Christopher Robin. They told him about
Eeyore's birthday.

"We want to give him a surprise party,"
said Pooh. "Those are more fun than other
kinds of parties."

"Yes, they are," said Christopher Robin.
"I will bring some chocolate cake."

"What about balloons?" asked Piglet.

Christopher Robin said he would also bring balloons.

Piglet and Pooh thanked him. Then they ran to see Owl before he went to sleep for the day.

Owl was glad to hear about the party.
"I can always stay awake for balloons and
chocolate cake," he said.

Kanga and Roo hopped along just then.
They also wanted to come to the party.
"We will wish Eeyore a very happy
birthday—even if it turns out not to be his
birthday after all," said Kanga.

Tigger bounced up. Pooh told him about
the party. Tigger grinned a tiggerish grin.
"There is nothing nicer than a party," he said.
"It will put some bounce into Eeyore."

Gopher popped out of the ground.
"Party?" he asked. "What party?"
"A birthday party for Eeyore," said Pooh.
"In case it is his birthday," said Piglet.
"I'll go! I'll go!" said Gopher.

Rabbit hopped by. It was he who thought of presents. "One always brings presents to a birthday party," he said. "It is the proper thing to do."

"Presents?" said Tigger. "Tiggers don't have money for presents."

"Bears don't either," said Pooh.

"We don't need money," said Kanga.
"We can have a sharing party. We can each
bring something we love. We can share that
thing with Eeyore. Then Eeyore will know we
love him. That is the important thing!"

Kanga said she would share her new umbrella with Eeyore. "It is red," she said. "That is a cheerful color. And an umbrella is useful even if it does not rain. It keeps off the sun."

"I will share my new sweater with Eeyore," said Roo. "It is red too. It will go with the umbrella."

"I will share my new ball," said Piglet.
"Eeyore can play with it at the party."
"He can bounce on my pogo stick when he is not playing with the ball," said Tigger.

"And when he is tired, he can sit in my
rocking chair," said Owl.

"I had a fine carrot crop this year," said Rabbit. "I will share my carrots with Eeyore."

"I will share my new shovel," said Gopher. "If Eeyore wants to dig a hole, he can use my shovel to do it!"

"What about you, dear Pooh?" asked
Kanga. "What will you share with Eeyore?"

For a minute Pooh looked unhappy. He
didn't own an umbrella or a sweater. He had
no pogo stick and no shovel. And he had no
chair. Pooh Bear had only one thing to share.

"I will bring my honey pot," said Pooh at last. "The good honey pot. The one that is almost full."

"Won't Eeyore be surprised!" said Kanga.

Then Kanga hurried home to get her umbrella.

Roo followed her.

Gopher went for his shovel.

All of Eeyore's friends ran off to get the things for the sharing party.

Then they set out, one by one, for Eeyore's house.

Piglet was trotting along with his ball when he met Eeyore on the path.

"Hello, little Piglet," said Eeyore. "Stop a bit and talk with me."

Piglet did not want to give away the surprise. "Look, Eeyore!" he said. "A fine big thistle!"

Eeyore was fond of thistles, so he looked. Piglet ran away as fast as he could go.

"Piglet does not want to talk with me," said Eeyore sadly. "I was foolish to think that he would."

Then Kanga and Roo came along.
Eeyore began to feel better. Kanga always
had time to talk to an old gray donkey.
But not today.
"We must hurry away, Eeyore," said
Kanga. "We are going to have tea with a
dear friend." She and Roo hurried on.

A tear ran down Eeyore's face. "That is how friends are sometimes," he said. "Here today and gone today."

Then Eeyore saw Pooh.

"Pooh Bear!" said Eeyore. "How nice to see you!"

"Dear, dear," said Pooh. He did not know what to do. "Oh! Eeyore, I can't stop now. I am on my way to the meadow to see where the bees keep their honey. That is why I have my honey pot, in case you wanted to know."

"What did I expect?" said poor Eeyore.
"Why should Pooh stop to visit with a gloomy
old donkey?"

"Why indeed, Eeyore?" said Christopher Robin. He had come quietly along the path. "Everyone is busy. Important things are happening—and I think they are happening at your house. If I were you, I would go home and see about it."

"At my house?" said Eeyore. "But nothing ever happens at my house." Just the same, he ran home.

All his friends were there. "Surprise!" they shouted. "Happy birthday, Eeyore! Surprise! Surprise!"

Eeyore was so happy that he did not know what to say.

Soon Christopher Robin came with cake and ice cream. Everyone sang and laughed, except for Eeyore. He almost smiled, though. And everyone wished Eeyore a happy birthday all over again.

Then the sharing began.
First Gopher showed Eeyore how to use the shovel.
"I think I am going to like sharing," said Eeyore.

He put on Roo's sweater and wore it for
a cap. It was so small, there was no other
way it would fit.

He sat in Owl's chair while Kanga put up
the red umbrella. It kept the sun off Eeyore
while he nibbled Rabbit's carrots.

He played with Piglet's ball. He bounced
on Tigger's pogo stick—but only Tiggers know
how to bounce properly! Then he had some
of Pooh's delicious honey. Why, Eeyore looked
almost happy!

When the party was over, everyone started for home. Pooh took his honey pot. It was half empty. But he did not care. At least, he did not care very much. "I feel so warm and happy inside. Is this what sharing does for a bear?" he wondered aloud.

"It is what sharing does for everyone,"
said Christopher Robin. "You are a good
bear, Pooh. When we get home I will fill your
honey pot again."

"I was hoping you would say that," said
Pooh with a happy sigh.

Pooh smiled when he thought of Eeyore's almost happy face. He began to hum. It was so nice to share. It was even nicer when one had a friend like Christopher Robin. He understood about honey pots and bears.